For Hannah and James

Kayla Liv
- enjoy the story!
Theadora

THE SAND TURTLE

Theadora Whittington

mccmcreations

It was a warm summer's day. Ben and his older sister, Ellie, were on a beach. But Ellie didn't want to play and Ben was getting

BORED! I want something exciting to

He could see that
his sister had
NO good ideas
so he gave up waiting
for her and started

to dig.

When he had
finished, he called

'IT'S A

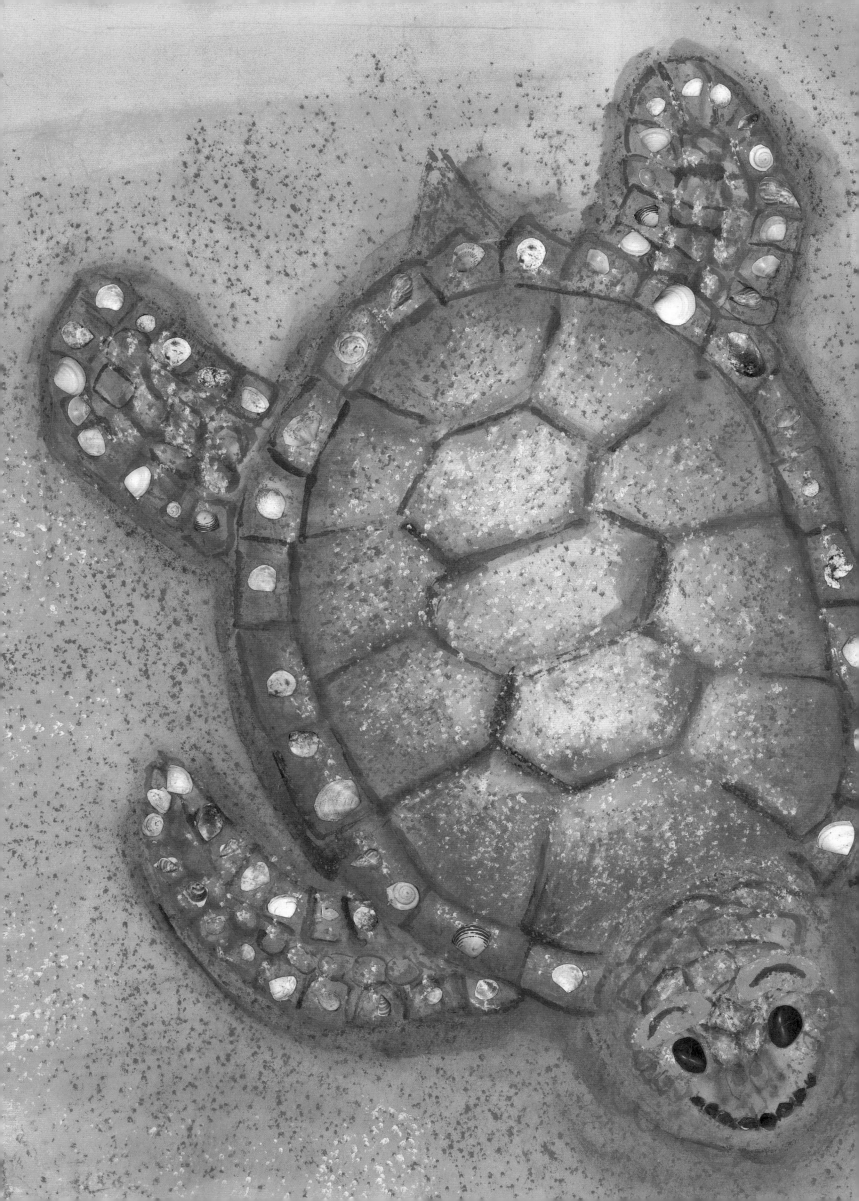

TURTLE!

He's WONDERFUL—
He's my friend,
and I want to play
with him.

'I wonder what kind of turtle he is,' said Ellie.

'Oh, I know! He's **very rare. He's a green turtle.** We must look after him,' Ben answered.

'I wonder if he'd like something good to eat. What have we in here?'

A chicken wing?

A banana?

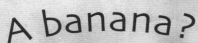

'I know what to get!'

But the turtle did not look pleased.

thought Ben.

'Would you like an ICE CREAM?' asked Ben

But the turtle didn't look **any** happier about that.

'Well really!' sighed Ben, 'What do you eat?'

'Since he's a green turtle, try offering him something GREEN?' suggested Ellie.

Ben brought
the turtle

some SEAWEED!

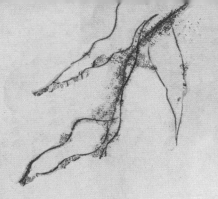

The turtle looked **extremely** pleased *now*.

'What a **strange** creature,' Ben remarked.

'He likes seaweed **more than ICE CREAM?'**

'Are you a green turtle because you eat **green food?**' Ben asked.

'**NO!**' laughed the turtle.
'If you look **really** carefully

at my tummy

you will see that I am a bit green there.

That's why I am a green turtle.
But I do like the taste of all those
green vegetables so many children
seem **not** to like!'

'Odd way to be,' replied Ben,
'I'll always prefer ice cream much
more than green vegetables.
Still, though we are very different,
we are special friends.'

The turtle nodded, 'I like it here
in the sun talking to you.'
But the turtle could also see that
THE TIDE

... was coming in.

Ben jumped up.

'Come and help,' he cried.

Together they tried to rescue the turtle,

BUT THE WAVES

... were approaching.

Ellie called, 'We must go!'

Ben looked back toward the waves. He looked really hard, and was astonished to see that the turtle was SWIMMING!

'What an amazing creature,' Ben thought.

And **then** he heard the turtle call to them ...

I like to swim!

'Don't be unhappy.
I shall swim on a long journey to a beautiful land,
a beach far away.'

'I will remember you!' Ben called back.

'I will remember you too. Will you do
something really kind for me?'
asked the turtle.

'If I can!' replied Ben.

'Will you return to this beach tomorrow and build another very special green turtle in the sand?' asked the turtle.

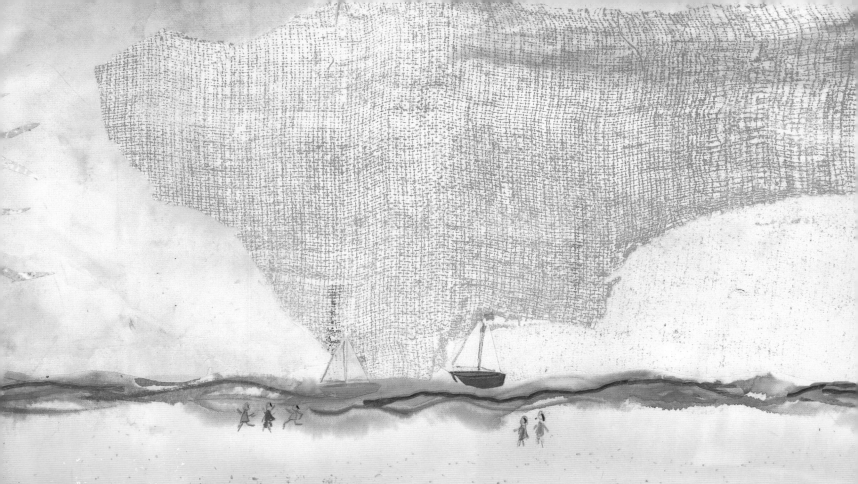

And the next day Ben and Ellie

created another turtle in the sand.

Put shells on your very own turtle and

give him something to eat.